RAGGEDY ANN AND ANDY
and the
Camel *with the* Wrinkled Knees

OTHER YEARLING BOOKS YOU WILL ENJOY:

Raggedy Ann Stories, JOHNNY GRUELLE

Raggedy Andy Stories, JOHNNY GRUELLE

Raggedy Ann and the Wonderful Witch
JOHNNY GRUELLE

Winnie-the-Pooh, A. A. MILNE

When We Were Very Young, A. A. MILNE

Now We Are Six, A. A. MILNE

The House at Pooh Corner, A. A. MILNE

The Wind in the Willows, KENNETH GRAHAME

Thimble Summer, ELIZABETH ENRIGHT

The Secret Garden, FRANCES HODGSON BURNETT

YEARLING BOOKS are designed especially to entertain and en-
lighten young people. The finest available books for children
have been selected under the direction of Charles F. Reasoner,
Professor of Elementary Education, New York University.

For a complete listing of all Yearling titles,
write to Education Sales Department, Dell Publishing Co., Inc.
1 Dag Hammarskjold Plaza, New York, N.Y. 10017.

RAGGEDY ANN
AND ANDY
and the
Camel *with the* Wrinkled Knees

WRITTEN
AND
ILLUSTRATED
by
JOHNNY GRUELLE

A YEARLING BOOK

Published by
DELL PUBLISHING CO., INC.
1 Dag Hammarskjold Plaza
New York, New York 10017

Yearling ® TM 913705, Dell Publishing Co., Inc.

ISBN: 0-440-47390-X

Reprinted by arrangement with The Bobbs-Merrill Company, Inc.

Printed in the United States of America

First Yearling printing—August 1977

Dedicated to
MARCELLA MATTHEWS

RAGGEDY ANN AND ANDY
AND THE CAMEL WITH
THE WRINKLED KNEES

Raggedy Ann and Raggedy Andy lay in their little doll beds, smiling up through the dark at the top of the play-house. It was very still and quiet in the play-house, but the Raggedys were not even a teeny-weeny speck lonesome, for they were thinking so many nice kindly thoughts. And, you know, when one thinks only lovely, kindly thoughts there is no time to become lonesome.

The play-house was an old piano-box and was all fixed up nice and cozy. There was an old rug upon the floor, two doll-beds, three little chairs, a table with pretty little play teacups and saucers and plates on it.

Raggedy Ann and Raggedy Andy lay upon

the doll beds just where Marcella had left them that afternoon. One of Raggedy Ann's legs was twisted up over the other, but it wasn't the least bit uncomfortable, for Raggedy Ann's legs were stuffed with nice white, soft cotton and they could be twisted in every position and it did not trouble Raggedy Ann. No indeed! Neither Raggedy Ann nor Raggedy Andy had moved since they had been placed in the little doll beds, and now it was late at night. Marcella had forgotten to take the Raggedys in the house, but the Raggedys did not mind that either. They just smiled up at the top of the play-house and listened to the tiny sounds which came from the little creatures out in the grass and flowers.

At first Raggedy Ann was so busy thinking nice kindly thoughts she did not notice. Then when Johnny Cricket stopped squeeking upon his tiny fiddle Raggedy Ann knew something was about to happen. Her little candy heart with the words "I love you" printed upon it went pitty-pat against her nice cotton-stuffed body. And Raggedy Ann heard great big footsteps coming up the path, "Thump! thump! thump."

"Hmm!" Raggedy Ann whispered to Raggedy Andy, "I wonder who that can be?"

The great big footsteps came up to the play-house and went on, "Thump! thump! thump!"

Raggedy Andy jumped out of the little doll-bed and tip-toed to the door. The night was dark, but Raggedy Andy had two very good shoe-button eyes and as they were black shoe-button eyes, Raggedy Andy could see very well in the dark. And what do you think? Raggedy Andy saw a great big man reach right in one of the windows to the house and take something and run! The man ran right by the piano-box play-house and Raggedy Andy could have jumped out and touched him if he had wished. But Raggedy Andy was so surprised to see anyone reach in another person's house and take something, he could think of nothing to do or say; and so the man jumped over the back fence and ran across the field!

"Did you see, Raggedy Ann?" Raggedy Andy asked.

"Yes!" said Raggedy Ann, very decidedly, "we must run up to the house and find out what that man was doing!"

So, smoothing the wrinkles out of her apron and jiggling her legs to get the twists out of them, Raggedy Ann and Raggedy Andy ran up to the house and climbed upon a chair so that they could peep over the sill into the window.

When Raggedy Ann and Raggedy Andy peeped up over the window-sill, all the dolls remained very quiet, for they thought it was the man returning; but when they saw that it was Raggedy Ann's and Raggedy Andy's faces

11

peeping in at them, they all jumped up and ran to them.

"What do you think, Raggedy Ann?" Uncle Clem cried. "Someone reached into the window and took the French doll! Wasn't that a rude thing to do?"

"My! My! My!" was all Raggedy Ann could say for awhile. Then after she sat and pulled her rag forehead down into a lot of wrinkles, Raggedy Ann was able to think of something to do.

"Raggedy Andy!" said Raggedy Ann. "We must run after the man and make him bring the French doll back here!"

"That is just what I was thinking!" Raggedy Andy replied, as he climbed upon the window-sill. "Come on, Raggedy Ann!"

Little Henny, the Dutch doll, wanted to go with Raggedy Ann and Raggedy Andy, but Raggedy Ann said, "No Henny, you must stay here and take care of the rest of the dolls! You see, you are the only man left!" This pleased

Henny so much he tried to stick out his chest so far that he fell over backwards and cried, "M-a-m-m-a!" in his quavery voice.

Raggedy Andy knew just which way the strange man had run, for he had watched him, so after jumping from the window and catching hold of her hand, Raggedy Andy and Raggedy Ann raced through the yard, climbed through a hole in the fence and scooted across the field.

Raggedy Ann and Raggedy Andy ran until they came to the center of the field, and all the way they had followed the man's trail where he had bent down the grass and field flowers. But when they came to the center of the field, the grass and flowers were not bent down, and Raggedy Ann and Raggedy Andy stopped.

"Now isn't that strange, Raggedy Ann?" Raggedy Andy asked. "He hasn't gone beyond here and still he isn't here!"

"Then if he isn't here," Raggedy Ann answered, "he must have gone on, Raggedy Andy."

"But how could he, Raggedy Ann, when we can see that his footsteps end right here?" Raggedy Andy asked.

"Why! He must have gone up in the air, that's what, Raggedy Andy!" Raggedy Ann replied.

"Then we can follow him no farther!" Raggedy Andy cried, as he dropped his rag arms to his side and looked very sad. "What shall we do, Raggedy Ann?"

"Let's sit down and think as hard as we can, Raggedy Andy," said Raggedy Ann. "Even if we rip sixteen stitches out of our heads thinking so hard, let's try to think of what we had better do."

So Raggedy Andy sat down beside her and threw one arm about Raggedy Ann's shoulder. And there they sat and thought and thought, just as hard as they could, until Raggedy Andy felt five stitches rip in his rag head and Raggedy Ann felt five stitches rip in her rag head, but neither one could think of anything to do.

"For," Raggedy Ann said out loud, "if we can't fly, how can we follow him?" This also puzzled Raggedy Andy and he said so.

Then Raggedy Ann and Raggedy Andy held their breaths; for, coming towards them through the flowers and tall grasses they saw a dim, greenish blue light. And as the pretty light (it

14

was just like a Will-o'the wisp) came up to them they saw that a pretty Fairy carried it at the end of a waving stick! No wonder Raggedy Ann and Raggedy Andy held their breaths, she was such a pretty little Fairy creature and it seemed so strange that at last they were getting to see a real for-sure live Fairy. Very often all the dolls had wished that they might see a Fairy. Now a very lovely Fairy stood before Raggedy Ann and Raggedy Andy! May be, very often, beautiful Fairies stand in front of us and whisper to us but we are unable to see or hear them; who knows? But Raggedy Ann and Raggedy Andy could not only see this pretty little Fairy creature, but they could hear her too.

"Why do you hold your breaths, Raggedy Ann and Raggedy Andy?" the pretty little Fairy asked, and there was a sly little tinkle to her voice which made Raggedy Ann and Raggedy Andy know that the pretty little Fairy knew why they held their breaths.

But Raggedy Ann laughed and said, "We are holding our breaths, because we have never seen a real for-sure live beautiful Fairy before, and we did not wish to frighten you away." And this made the pretty little Fairy laugh right out loud.

"Of course, I knew why, Raggedy Ann and Raggedy Andy," she said. "But now that we are good friends, please do not hold your breaths any longer. For, I know why you are sitting out in

the center of the field and I know just how you can follow the man who took the French doll."

"I thought maybe the man might be Santa Claus," Raggedy Ann said. "But then after I had ripped five stitches in my rag head thinking, I knew it could not be Santa who took the French doll, for he only takes dolls when they need fixing up and the French doll was always kept just as good as new. Except when Marcella fed her chocolate candy and got chocolate around the French doll's mouth."

"No, it wasn't Santa Claus," Raggedy Andy said.

"No, it wasn't Santa Claus," the pretty little Fairy agreed. "But now the thing to do is for you two to follow the strange man. And in order to do that, you must be able to fly, for he flew away from here, you know."

"That is just what I thought," Raggedy Ann said.

"Raggedy Ann can think ever so much better than I can," Raggedy Andy told the Fairy. "For Raggedy Ann has a lovely candy heart and I guess that's why."

The pretty little Fairy laughed at this and said, "Granny Balloon-spider lives near here and I will ask her to build you a nice fluffy balloon so that you can follow the man who took the French doll." And the pretty little Fairy led the way until they came to a cunning little cottage and there stood Granny out on the porch waiting for them.

"Will you spin Raggedy Ann and Raggedy Andy a nice fluffy balloon in which they can fly after the man who took the French doll?" the pretty little Fairy asked Granny.

"Indeed, I will be very glad to spin them a balloon!" Granny replied. "But in order to carry

18

them through the air I will have to spin such a large balloon that it will take me several days."

"Oh, I shall fix that all right, Granny," the pretty little Fairy laughed. "If you will bring your little spinning-wheel out here on the porch, I will say a magic charm over it, and you will be able to spin the balloon in a very short time!"

So, when Granny Balloon-spider brought the cunning little spinning-wheel out upon the porch, the pretty little Fairy waved her fairy light over it and sang, "Little cunning spinning-wheel, spin and whir and sing, spin a silken balloon to carry Raggedy Ann and Raggedy Andy up in the air in search of the French doll!" And Granny put her little red-slippered foot upon the treadle of the spinning-wheel and the cunning little spinning-wheel looked like solid silver it whirled so fast. And before you could recite, "The house that Jack built" the little silken balloon was finished.

The pretty little Fairy fastened a silken thread to Raggedy Ann's hand and to Raggedy Andy's hand and touched the silken balloon with her fairy light; then the silken balloon rose in the air and carried Raggedy Ann and Raggedy Andy with it.

"Good bye and thank you!" Raggedy Ann and Raggedy Andy called down to the little Fairy and Granny Balloon-spider, and the little Fairy waved her fairy light until the silken balloon had carried our two friends way up above a feathery cloud.

And as the gentle breeze blew them along, ever so gently, Raggedy Ann and Raggedy Andy

Johnny Gruelle

twisted and swung about at the end of the silken threads tied to their rag hands.

"Isn't it lovely, Raggedy Andy?" Raggedy Ann asked. "I can scarcely believe we are not dreaming!"

"It is ever so much nicer than floating on water!" Raggedy Andy replied.

CHAPTER TWO

Raggedy Ann and Raggedy Andy floated through the air, carried along by the silken balloon until they could see the great, round, golden Sun peeping up over the rim of the Earth.

"Good morning, Mr. Sun!" Raggedy Ann laughed; but of course the Sun did not answer, for he was thousands of miles away and did not hear. Then Raggedy Ann noticed that they were drifting closer and closer to the ground, and after awhile, the silken balloon caught in a low branch of a tree and there Raggedy Ann and Raggedy Andy hung, dangling by the silken cords the Fairy had tied to their hands.

"Well, here we are!" laughed Raggedy Andy, "But how will we get down to the ground?"

"That is what has been bothering me, too," Raggedy Ann said. "Of course it would not hurt

either of us to drop from here to the ground, if we could only untie the silken cords the Fairy tied about our hands."

And so Raggedy Ann and Raggedy Andy hung there dangling and twisting about until finally Raggedy Andy laughed and asked, "Do you know what, Raggedy Ann?"

"No, what, Raggedy Andy?" Raggedy Ann asked in reply.

"Why," Raggedy Andy said. "If we can't get down, then let's get up!" And with this, Raggedy Andy twisted his legs up over the limb and was soon sitting upon it. Then he pulled Raggedy Ann up beside him. When they had their hands in front of them, it was an easy matter to untie the silken cord.

"There we are!" laughed Raggedy Andy. "Now all we have to do, is to jump from the tree and continue our search for the French doll!" So Raggedy Ann and Raggedy Andy stood up on the limb and took hold of hands.

"One for the money, two for the show, three to make ready and here she goes!" they both sang and jumped. "Blump! Blump!" they struck against the ground and rolled over.

"Didn't hurt me a speck!" laughed Raggedy Ann.

"Me either!" laughed Raggedy Andy as he sat up and dusted his clothes.

"Ha!" came a voice from behind the tree, and as they looked Raggedy Ann and Raggedy Andy saw the queerest creature come walking towards them. It was a Camel, made out of canton flannel and stuffed with sawdust, but he had evidently been played with so much, his legs were no longer straight and stiff. Instead, the canton flannel Camel's legs were wrinkled and so out of press, it seemed that he would pitch forward upon his head at each step. When the Camel came up to Raggedy Ann and Raggedy Andy, he sat down beside them, and in doing this his knees gave way with him and he rolled over upon his side.

"Wup!" Raggedy Andy said, as he helped the Camel to sit up, "You almost fell over that time."

"Indeed I did," the Camel laughed, "My legs are not what they used to be. See how wrinkled my knees are?"

Raggedy Andy tried to smooth out the wrinkles in the Camel's knees, but the Camel smiled and said, "It doesn't do a bit of good trying to get the wrinkles out. They come right back in again just as soon as I stand up," he continued. "You see when I was brand-new, I was made with sticks in each leg, but these sticks were the sticks which are made to put in meat when it is tied up and roasted, and each stick had a point at the end. Well, sir, after I had been played with for a few weeks, those pointed sticks punched right up through my back and I wasn't safe for a little boy to play with. So the little boy's mother pulled the meat sticks out of my legs, and that let me sag down until my knees grew terribly wrinkled!"

"That is too bad!" Raggedy Ann said, as she patted the Camel's head.

"Four bad, my dear!" the Camel corrected.

"Oh, I didn't mean the number of legs you had, I meant that I felt sorry," Raggedy Ann laughed.

"Ha! Ha! Now I understand," the Camel laughed. "But really it isn't quite as bad as one would imagine, for when I had sticks in my legs I had to walk stiff-legged and that wasn't a speck graceful, but now, I can walk along very softly

26

without going 'thump! thump! thump!' And it is ever so much more comfortable when I lie down now than it was when I had to stick my legs out stiffly at the side."

"When you said, 'Thump! thump! thump!' it reminded me of something!" said Raggedy Ann.

"What was it?" the Camel with the wrinkled knees asked.

Then Raggedy Ann told him how she had heard the man's footsteps go "thump! thump! thump!" the night before.

The Camel with the wrinkled knees scratched his head with the loppiest leg and asked, "Was he a large man, with two legs and two arms, dressed in clothing?"

"The very man!" cried Raggedy Andy, "I was looking out of the play-house door when the man reached in the window and took her!"

"Then, I am sure I can tell you how to find him!" the Camel with the wrinkled knees cried, excitedly. "For I know it is the same man who took me out of the little boy's play-house one night. I ran away from him. Some day I'm going back home, for I had lots of good times with my little boy owner!"

"Hurry and tell us how to find the mean man, please!" Raggedy Ann begged. "For we must rescue the French doll and return home as soon as we can."

"Well," the Camel with the wrinkled knees

said, "Do you see that great big tree way over there?"

"Yes!" Raggedy Ann and Raggedy Andy both cried.

"Well," the Camel said. "You mustn't go that way! You must go this way. Then when you get to this way you must turn and go that way until you come to this way again. Then take the first turn this way, until you come to that way and after walking that way ten minutes you turn and go this way. Then you are there."

"Hmm!" mused Raggedy Ann and Raggedy

Andy, "We should be able to find it in the dark after such a *good* description of the way to reach there!"

"That's the funny part of the whole thing," the Camel with the wrinkled knees laughed. "I ran away from the man at night when it was very, very dark, and I could easily find my way back in the dark, but I would get lost in the daytime!"

"Then I guess we will have to go alone," Raggedy Ann said.

"I'd like to return with you and help rescue the French doll," the Camel with the wrinkled knees said. "But I know I should never be able to find it in the light."

"Maybe if you would shut your eyes you could lead us to the place where the man lives," Raggedy Andy suggested.

"Ha!" the Camel laughed, "How can I shut my eyes, when they are shoc buttons just like Raggedy Ann's?"

"I never thought of that!" Raggedy Andy said. "But be quiet—Raggedy Ann is trying to think of some way!"

"I never said a word!" the Camel replied.

"Yes, you did!" Raggedy Andy said. "You are talking now, and it disturbs Raggedy Ann while she is thinking! So please remain very quiet and don't even cough, because sometimes Raggedy Ann rips a great many stitches out of her head and the cotton stuffing shows after she has thought real, real hard. Just sit quietly and wait, as I am doing, and pretty soon you will be surprised to find out how well Raggedy Ann can think. Why, I remember one time when we were having a—"

"I shan't say a word!" the Camel promised.

"Yes, you say that you will not say anything, but just the minute you say that, can't you see that you are saying something?"

"Well! How can you tell that I shan't say a word unless I tell you that I shan't say a word? Just you tell me that, Mister Raggedy Andy!" the Camel replied.

"This is no time to guess riddles," Raggedy Andy said. "If we were guessing riddles, I know one I'll bet a nickel you could never, never guess. But what I have asked you to do is to remain very quiet, for the more quiet you remain the sooner Raggedy Ann will be able to think of something to do.

"Then I shall remain positively quiet, Raggedy Andy, so let's not quarrel about it."

"I shan't quarrel with you," Raggedy Andy replied, "But you continually start—"

"I've thought of a good scheme!" Raggedy Ann cried, as she jumped to her feet. "If the Camel with the wrinkled knees cannot shut his eyes and if he cannot show us the way to the man's place in the daytime, then we must cover

31

his eyes with a hanky. Then it will be just the same as if it were dark!"

"I only see one thing wrong with your idea, Raggedy Ann," the Camel said.

"What is it?" Raggedy Ann asked.

"Why," the Camel replied, "If we tie something over the man's eyes, don't you see we will be where he is without having to go there!"

"Silly!" Raggedy Andy cried, "Raggedy Ann means to tie something over your eyes instead of the man's eyes!"

"Oh!" the Camel with the wrinkled knees laughed, as Raggedy Ann tied her pocket hanky over the Camel's shoe-button eyes, "Now I see!"

When Raggedy Ann had finished tying her pocket hanky over the Camel's eyes she said, "Now we had better start."

"Turn me around three times," the Camel said. "So that I won't get all mixed up in my directions. Then you had better get upon my back, for I shall go just as fast as I possibly can and you may not be able to keep up with me."

Raggedy Ann turned the Camel with the wrinkled knees around three times, then she and Raggedy Andy climbed upon his back.

"Hold tight!" the Camel cried, "Here we go!" and with this he started walking, slowly at first, then faster and faster, until soon his wabbly, wrinkled legs were hitting the ground, "Clump-

ity clumpity, clumpity," and he was running surprisingly fast.

Raggedy Ann and Raggedy Andy held on, even though the Camel bounced them up and down a great deal as he jumped along.

"Where are we now?" the Camel asked, after he had run steadily for five minutes. Raggedy Ann and Raggedy Andy looked about them.

"Why!" they cried in surprise, "We are right back where we started from! You must have run in a large circle!"

"Maybe I did," the Camel replied, "Of course I cannot see where I am running, but I know perfectly well that I am going in the right direction."

"But, Mr. Camel!" Raggedy Ann exclaimed, as she slid from the Camel's back, "How can you be going in the right direction when you return to the place where we started from? Can't you see, that we might just as well have stood still and saved you all that running?"

"Maybe we had better try it again!" the Camel advised, "I am certain that I am not mistaken!"

So Raggedy Ann and Raggedy Andy again climbed upon the Camel's back and again the Camel carried them at a run for five minutes.

"Now where are we?" the Camel asked.

"We are right where we started from!" Rag-

gedy Andy cried, "I don't believe you know where you are trying to go!"

"Of course I don't!" the Camel agreed. "But do not let that fool you! I have run exactly the same as I did when I came from the man's place!"

"A-hhhhh!" Raggedy Ann exclaimed. "I know what's the trouble, Mr. Camel! You have been running just the same as you did when you came from the man's place so in order to return to the man's place, don't you see you must run backwards!"

"Of course!" the Camel chuckled. "It's funny I didn't think of running backwards before!" The Camel couldn't run quite as fast backwards as he did frontward, but he covered a lot of ground. After running backwards for five minutes, the Camel again asked, "Where are we now?"

"I do not know!" Raggedy Ann and Raggedy Andy both answered.

"Then," said the Camel, "We must be getting somewhere!"

CHAPTER THREE

When the Camel with the wrinkled knees had rested for a few minutes, he again started running backwards and was jumping along very fast when Raggedy Ann cried suddenly, "Whoa!"

The Camel immediately stopped and Raggedy Ann and Raggedy Andy, not expecting him to stop so suddenly, rolled off his back and turned over and over in the grass.

"Why did you cry, 'Whoa'?" the Camel wished to know when Raggedy Ann and Raggedy Andy had picked themselves up and came back to him.

"There's a little girl standing over there crying," Raggedy Ann said. "We must go over and see what is the trouble."

Raggedy Ann took the hanky from the Camel's eyes and the three walked over towards the little

girl. When the little girl saw them she stopped crying and said, "Don't come any closer, or the Snap Dragons will catch you!"

"Hmm," mused Raggedy Andy. "Snap Dragons—who's afraid of Snap Dragons? Not me!" And with that, he walked right up to the little girl.

Raggedy Ann, when she saw that nothing happened to Raggedy Andy, also walked up to the little girl.

"The Snap Dragons are nothing but flowers," Raggedy Andy said, and indeed this was true, for all about the little girl's feet pretty flowers were twined.

"How long have you been standing here, little girl?" Raggedy Ann asked.

"For a long, long time," the little girl replied. "Every time I try to walk away the Snap Dragons catch my feet and hold me."

"Nonsense!" Raggedy Andy exclaimed. "Catch hold of my hand and we will walk over to where there are no Snap Dragons!"

But when the little girl did this and Raggedy Andy tried to walk, he found that the Snap Dragons also fastened themselves around his legs.

And when Raggedy Ann caught hold of Raggedy Andy's hand and pulled, the Snap Dragons wrapped themselves around her feet and held her.

"You see!" the little girl cried, "Now you are prisoners too, and we will never get away from them!"

When the Camel saw that Raggedy Ann had become a prisoner too, he turned and walked still farther away from the Snap Dragons and sat down to think it over. Although the Camel with the wrinkled knees sat and tried to think for a long, long time, he could not think of a way to rescue his friends from the Snap Dragons. Even though he scratched his head with his left hind leg he could not think of a way.

"I wonder how long we will have to stay here before we are rescued?" Raggedy Ann mused out loud.

"We may have to stay here years and years!" the little girl cried. Then she told Raggedy Ann and Raggedy Andy all about herself. "My name is Jenny," the little girl began, "and my brother's name is Jan. We used to live in a little cottage right in the center of the deep, deep woods. The little cottage was no larger than a big dry-goods box, but that was large enough for Jan and me. You see, we lived there all by ourselves."

"Didn't you have a mamma or a daddy?" Raggedy Ann asked in surprise.

"No," Jenny replied, as she brushed a tear from her eye. "Mamma and Daddy went over to see Gran'ma one day, and they never came back.

So Jan and I went into the deep, deep woods to hunt for mamma and daddy, but we could not find them. And we could not find our way back home so when we discovered the dear little cottage, which was no larger than a dry-goods box, Jan and I lived there!"

"But where is Jan now?" Raggedy Andy wanted to know.

"I was just about to tell you!" Jenny replied. "In the deep, deep woods, as you surely must know, there are Gnomes and Elves and Fairies! And besides the Fairies and Gnomes and Elves there are other little creatures. Sometimes Jan and I could not see the little Fairies and Gnomes and Elves or other little creatures, but we could hear them singing, or laughing or talking. Then at other times, we could see them, but we could not hear them. Then sometimes we could see and hear them, too. And so, one day, Jan went out in back of the cunning little cottage to get a pail of water from the spring and when he came back into the house there was the queerest little man-creature with him we had ever seen!"

"What was it?" Raggedy Ann asked.

"It was a Loonie!" Jenny answered. "And if you have never seen a Loonie, do not ever long to see one, for they are not as cunning as Elves and Gnomes or Fairies! Instead, Loonies have large eyes which roll around every which way, and

long red noses and crooked legs. They are funny-looking little creatures and really make you laugh when you see them. And that is just what Jan and I did, when the little Loonie walked into our little house with Jan. And do you know?" Jenny said, "When we laughed at the little Loonie, it made him so angry, he just bounced all around our little house and yelled at us."

"I'll just bet, when you laughed at him, that made him hopping mad," said Raggedy Andy.

"Yes," Jenny said, "That is just what happened, and we did not know that such a small creature could be so strong. And before either Jan or I could do a thing, the little Loonie caught Jan's feet and dragged him right out of the little cottage and away through the woods!"

"Couldn't Jan catch hold of bushes, so the Loonie couldn't pull him?" Raggedy Andy asked.

"Oh, yes," Jenny replied. "But the little Loonie was so strong, he just pulled Jan's hands away from the bushes and ran with him so fast, I could not follow." And Jenny began crying again.

"Please do not cry," Raggedy Ann begged, as she wiped the little girl's eyes with her apron, "We will help you find Jan. And when we catch the Loonie we will spank him good. Won't we, Raggedy Andy?"

"Indeed we will," Raggedy Andy promised.

"And after I had searched and searched for Jan, all through the deep, deep woods, and could not find him, I came out across this field, and just the minute I stopped amongst the Snap Dragons, they twined around my feet and I could not move."

"And you have never found out where the Loonie took Jan?" Raggedy Ann asked.

"I suppose he took Jan to the Town of the Loonies," Jenny answered. "But even though I

44

asked everyone I met in the deep woods, they could not tell me how to get to Loonie Town."

"Perhaps someone could have told you," Raggedy Ann suggested. "But maybe they knew that if you went there alone, you would be captured and made a prisoner just as Jan was."

Jenny was just about to reply to Raggedy Ann when she saw a funny old Horse, not much larger than the Camel with the wrinkled knees.

"What are you all standing around for?" the old Horse asked as he came up to the edge of the patch of Snap Dragons. "Is there going to be a parade?"

"You'd better come over here and sit down with me," the Camel with the wrinkled knees called. "I am trying to think."

The old Horse walked over to where the Camel sat and lay down beside him. "My, I'm tired," the Horse sighed.

"Have you walked far?" the Camel with the wrinkled knees asked.

"No, not very far," the old Horse replied, "but you see, I am so old, the least bit of exercise wears me out and I have to lie down and rest."

"I am trying to think of a way to rescue my friends there," the Camel said, as he pointed to Raggedy Ann, Raggedy Andy and Jenny.

"Have they been captured?" the tired old Horse wanted to know.

"Certainly," the Camel replied, "They are

standing right in a whole lot of Snap Dragons and can't get away."

"Hmm," the tired old Horse said, as he slowly got to his feet and stretched, "I will look into this." And from his pants pocket he took a case and from the case a pair of old-fashioned spectacles.

When he had put the spectacles on his nose he walked up and looked at the Snap Dragons. "Well, I'll declare!" he cried as he jumped back suddenly and upset the Camel. "Just put on my spectacles," he said, as he handed them to the Camel.

When the Camel with the wrinkled knees had the spectacles on his nose and looked at the Snap Dragons, he turned and ran as hard as his wobbly legs would let him. And the tired old Horse ran after him. After an exciting chase clear across the field, the tired old Horse finally managed to catch the Camel's string tail between his teeth and stop him.

"Silly!" the tired old Horse cried, as he took his spectacles away from the Camel, "I didn't mean to give you the spectacles to keep. I just

48

loaned them to you." And the tired old Horse placed the spectacles on his own nose and slowly walked back towards Raggedy Ann and the others.

"I did not mean to keep your spectacles," the Camel with the wrinkled knees tried to explain, as he followed the tired old Horse.

"Then why did you run?" the tired old Horse asked, "That's what I want to know."

"Because," the camel replied. "Those are not Snap Dragon flowers at all! They are real live Dragons! Chinese Dragons!"

The tired old Horse turned and looked the Camel with the wrinkled knees up and down, from his feet to his head. Then shaking his head sadly the tired old Horse walked amongst the Snap Dragons and laid down.

"Now you are in a pickle too!" Raggedy Andy cried. "How can you rescue us when you are captured just the same as we are?"

The tired old Horse rolled over upon his back and kicked his four feet in the air, "If I can roll all the way over, I'm worth a hundred dollars," he said.

"I wouldn't give five cents for you now!" the

Camel cried, as he sat down at the edge of the clump of Snap Dragons.

After kicking about for a few minutes, the tired old Horse succeeded in rolling over. "Whee!" the tired old Horse cried, "I'm worth a hundred dollars!" and with that he began prancing and kicking up his heels and frisking all about Raggedy Ann and Raggedy Andy and Jenny.

"You be careful there, Mister," Raggedy Ann cautioned, "First thing you know, you'll kick Jenny!"

CHAPTER FOUR

The tired old Horse stopped kicking up his heels and walked up to Jenny and looked at her intently through his spectacles. Then he took them off and wiped them with a red bandanna handkerchief. "Ha!" he cried, when he looked at Jenny without his spectacles, "I thought I recognized you. You used to live in the little cottage in the center of the deep, deep woods, didn't you?"

"Why, yes," Jennie replied. "How did you know?"

"Because," the tired old Horse said, "I used to be driven through the deep, deep woods every day, to haul wood for my master until I got so old and tired I couldn't haul wood any more; then my master turned me loose to live by myself

and he got a young horse to take my place. I used to see you almost every day. You and Jan," the Horse continued. "Why don't you return to the cunning little cottage?"

"Because," Raggedy Andy replied, "can't you see, Jenny has been captured by the Snap Dragons, and so have we, and so have you."

"Nonsense!" the tired old Horse laughed. "All

you have to do is just walk away from the Snap
Dragons like this."

"Huh!" the Camel with the wrinkled knees
cried, when he saw that the tired old Horse
couldn't budge. "Now you are in for it, just like
the rest of them."

The tired old Horse looked at his feet and all

about him in a surprised sort of way. Then a broad smile spread over his kindly face and he put on his spectacles. When the spectacles were firmly placed upon his nose, the Horse ran in circles around Raggedy Ann, Raggedy Andy and Jenny.

"There! You see?" the tired old Horse said, as he stopped in front of Jenny, "I couldn't budge before, because I did not have on my magic spectacles, and the Snap Dragons looked just like Snap Dragons! But now that I have on my Magic spectacles, the Snap Dragons are only Violets, so of course they can not get around my feet and hold me!"

"Then will we have to wear magic spectacles before we can get away from the Snap Dragons?" Jenny wished to know.

"Oh, no," the tired old Horse replied, "I shall eat all the Violets which look to you like Snap Dragons. In that way, I shall have a fine meal and they won't tangle around your feet." And without another word, the tired old Horse started eating, and in a short time Jenny was able to walk over and sit down beside the Camel with the wrinkled knees.

"My, goodness," she said, "It feels good to be able to sit down again."

It did not take the tired old Horse very long to eat the Violets around Raggedy Ann's and Raggedy Andy's feet and so, very soon, they were all standing together beside the Camel with the wrinkled knees.

The tired old Horse took off his spectacles and put them in his pocket.

"Now," he said, as he rubbed his forefeet together, just as a man does when he is about to say something interesting. "We will talk about Jenny and Jan."

"We must help Jenny find Jan, don't you think so?" Raggedy Ann asked.

"Indeed, that is just what I was going to say!" cried the tired old Horse. "When I used to haul wood through the deep, deep woods past Jenny's little cottage I used to see her and Jan playing there together almost every day."

"But I do not remember seeing you," Jenny laughed.

"There was a good reason, my dear," the tired old Horse laughed. "At that time I was just an ordinary horse and you belong to some tribe of Fairies, or Gnomes, or Elves, or something. Anyway, I could see you, but you could not see me, nor could you see my master or the cart of wood I used to haul. Could you?"

"No. I do not remember seeing the cart, or your master," Jennie replied.

"There, you see!" the tired old Horse said to Raggedy Ann. "Well, one day I was hauling wood for my master and I saw the Loonie come out of your little cottage dragging Jan. And although I wanted to run after the Loonie and rescue Jan, I could not do so, because I was hitched to the cart. But I watched until I saw right where the Loonie took Jan, and I'll bet sixteen nickels I can show you right where he took Jan inside a great tree."

"Then let us waste no time in going there!" Raggedy Andy cried, as he jumped to his feet. "There is no telling, perhaps Jan has been in prison all this time."

"I will take Jenny upon my back, because she is the heaviest and the Camel can take Raggedy Ann and Raggedy Andy upon his back, and we will run like everything until we come to the deep, deep woods."

"But," said the Camel with the wrinkled knees, "I was taking Raggedy Ann and Raggedy Andy to show them where the man had taken the French Doll. And the only way I can find the place is to be blindfolded and run backwards, and if I do that, how can I follow you, Mister Horse?"

"I tell you what let's do," Raggedy Ann suggested. "Let us do as the tired old Horse says, then when we rescue Jan from the Loonies, we will all search for the man who carried away the French doll, Babette."

This was agreeable to the Camel with the

wrinkled knees and soon he and the tired old Horse were racing across the fields towards the deep, deep woods. In a few moments they came to the deep, deep woods and raced down a winding path until they came to the little cottage where Jenny and Jan lived. And a few yards beyond this, the tired old Horse sat down under a great tree.

"Whew!" he cried, as he took off his hat and fanned himself, "That surely made me tired! Well, anyway, here is the tree in which the Loonie took Jan."

"And if I am not mistaken," the Camel with the wrinkled knees said, "this is also the place

where I was running backwards to. Just put your handkerchief over my eyes and let me see."

When Raggedy Ann had bound her handkerchief over the Camel's eyes, he said, "Yes, sir, this is the very spot!" And he handed Raggedy Ann her hanky.

"What I can't understand is how the Loonie could drag Jan into the tree when there isn't a single hole in the tree," Raggedy Andy said. Everyone walked around the large tree, but there appeared no hole of any sort in the tree.

"Are you sure you haven't made a mistake, Mister Horse?" Raggedy Andy asked.

"I am sure," the tired old Horse replied. "And besides, doesn't the Camel say this is the place he was trying to run to?"

The tired old Horse took off his hat again and scratched his head. "Ah," he said, "I have it. We must blindfold the Camel with the wrinkled knees and follow him into the tree; for I am sure it is a magic tree, or at least the entrance into the tree is covered with magic and we are unable to see it."

So Raggedy Ann again blindfolded the Camel with the wrinkled knees and without waiting for the others, he backed into the tree and disappeared. And where the Camel with the wrinkled knees had backed into the tree, there was no hole of any sort to be seen.

"O, dear!" Raggedy Ann cried when the last

of the Camel disappeared into the tree. "Now he has gone and we shall be unable to follow!"

For as she spoke she walked up to where the Camel had disappeared and felt of the tree; it was just as solid there as at any other place upon its surface.

"We should all have held onto the Camel's nose," the Horse said. "For I guess there is something magic about the Camel which lets him walk through things when he is blindfolded."

"I guess there is nothing to do except wait outside here until the Camel finds we are not with him. Then perhaps he will return," Raggedy Andy said. Presently the Camel poked his head out of the tree trunk. "Where are you?" he asked.

"Right where you left us," Raggedy Ann replied. "Let us all catch hold of your nose and perhaps we can all get into the tree." And when everyone had crowded around the Camel and had caught hold of his nose, the Camel backed into the tree and the others went with him.

The tree seemed very much larger, when our friends were once inside, and appeared as a great room. Over at one side of the great room there was a slab of stone with a ring in it.

"It must be a trap-door," Raggedy Andy said as he caught hold of the ring and tired to raise the stone.

"Let us all catch hold of the ring," Raggedy

Ann suggested. "Perhaps we can lift it." But though all pulled with all their might, the stone would not be lifted.

"This must be the way down into Loonie Land," the tired old Horse said. "Let us sit down and see what we can think of. There must be a way to open this trap-door."

And as he finished speaking, the tired old Horse sat down upon the stone. And as he sat down rather hard, the stone lowered with him and he went tumbling down below. The others could not see where the tired old Horse fell to, for the stone immediately closed after he had disappeared, but they could hear him bumping around until he reached the bottom.

"I hope it did not hurt him," Raggedy Ann said. "Listen!"

They could hear the tired old Horse kicking around way down below. And presently they heard his footsteps as he came climbing up.

"Are you there?" the tired old Horse called up through the stone trap-door.

"Yes," Raggedy Ann replied. "What shall we do?"

"I took a peachy tumble," the Horse called back. "If you just press down gently upon the stone, I am sure it will open." And indeed, this proved correct, for when Raggedy Andy pressed down ever so lightly, the stone lowered and they

could see the tired old Horse standing upon the stone steps.

"Come on," he said, "I will hold the stone trap-door open until you all get it. But watch you don't slip on the stone steps, for it is a long way to the bottom."

"That ring was just up in the top of the stone to fool anyone who came into the tree," Raggedy

Andy said when all had safely reached the bottom of the stone steps. "For the ring made it look as though you had to pull on the trap-door to open it."

"I am glad that it was I who sat upon the stone instead of Jenny," the tired old Horse laughed.

CHAPTER FIVE

A wonderful sight met their eyes, when the tired old Horse opened a door at the bottom of the stone steps and our friends walked out into the open again. There, in the distance, upon a wonderful hill, stood a beautiful castle with turrets and spires of red reaching up towards the sky. And between our friends and the castle, there was a large valley filled with strangely-shaped little houses. From where they stood, Raggedy Ann and Raggedy Andy, Jenny, the tired old Horse and the Camel with the wrinkled knees could see the Loonies running about in the streets like mad. First running one way and then running another.

"What's the matter with them, I wonder?" the tired old Horse said. Of course neither Jenny or any of her friends knew the reason, so they could

not answer. But soon the Loonies all came running towards them shouting and waving sticks.

"I believe that they see us," said the Camel, who had removed the blindfold from his eyes.

This was true, for the queer little Loonies came swarming towards them, looking for all the world like ants as they crossed the valley.

"Where can we hide?" Jenny asked, as she looked about her.

"We shan't hide!" Raggedy Andy cried. "We will wait and see what they intend doing."

The Loonies soon showed our friends what they intended doing, for they all surrounded Raggedy Ann and Jenny and Raggedy Andy and the tired old Horse and the Camel with the wrinkled

knees, and poking them with their sticks, started marching our friends down into the valley towards the queer houses.

"Do you think it would be a good plan for me to start kicking?" the tired old Horse whispered to Raggedy Ann. "I can knock them head-over-heels if I start kicking and thrashing about."

"I do not believe I would do that," Raggedy Ann replied. "For your heels are hard and you would hurt them very much should you kick any of the Loonies."

"All right," the tired old Horse agreed. "Then we will march along quietly."

The Loonies marched their prisoners into the largest house in the center of all the other queer houses and up before the King of the Loonies.

"Aha!" the Loonie King cried, when all the Loonies had stopped their chattering. "What have we captured?"

One of the Loonies who had captured our friends spoke and said to the Loonie King, "Oh, most Looniest of Loonies, we have captured those who came down through the great tree."

"Don't I know that?" the Loonie King howled. "Why don't you answer my question? Whom have we captured?"

"We have captured the prisoners," the Loonie Guard replied.

"Good!" the Loonie King cried, as he clapped his hands. "Now see if you can answer this one.

What will we do with them now that we have captured them?"

"Put them in prison, I guess," the Guard replied.

"Wrong!" shouted the Loonie King. "Now try to think!"

"I can't seem to think of anything," the Guard answered.

"Good!" the Loonie King again clapped his hands together. "You guessed that I was thinking that I couldn't think of anything either! Now here is another and this is the hardest of all. What is the name of that man with the funny hat?" And the Loonie King pointed his long finger at the Horse.

The tired old Horse looked around at his friends and winked one eye. "He called me a man," he giggled.

"Please remain quiet when I am asking riddles!" the Loonie King shouted at the Horse.

"His name is Spoogledoogle," the Guard said.

"Good!" the Loonie King again cried as he clapped his hands. "That is right."

"It is wrong," the tired old Horse said.

"It is right!" the Loonie King cried. "Whatever I say is right, *is* right, whether it is right or wrong!"

"All right," the tired old Horse replied. "I shall not argue with you, but I know that I am not a Spoogledoogle, for there isn't any such animal!" And with this, the tired old Horse walked over and laid down in a small flower garden at one side of the room.

"Here!" the Loonie King shouted at the tired old Horse. "Get out of that flower bed! You are worse than the neighbor's chickens!" The tired old Horse made no reply, but put his head down upon the prettiest flowers and went to sleep. The Loonie King took off his crown and scratched his head. "Do all Spoogledoogles act that way?" he finally asked Raggedy Ann.

"Oh yes," Raggedy Ann replied, with a twinkle in her shoe-button eyes. "If you watch him for awhile, you will see that when he gets up he will be a Horse instead of a Spoogledoogle." And Jenny and Raggedy Andy snickered behind their hands.

The Loonie King looked doubtfully at Raggedy Ann. "Why did you come to The Loonie Land?" he asked.

"We came in search of Jan," Raggedy Ann replied, "One of the Loonies carried him away from his sister, and we are searching for him."

"Hmm!" the Loonie King mused as he rubbed his chin. "Now I must try and fool you. My Loonie did not catch Jan near the little cottage in the deep, deep woods and drag him down here."

"Oh!" Raggedy Ann cried as she put her hands to her face. "What a fib!"

"How do you know it's a fib?" the Loonie King asked.

"Because," Raggedy Ann replied. "If the Loonie did not do that, how do you know he

caught Jan near the little cottage in the deep, deep woods?"

"That's so," the Loonie King agreed. "Well, anyway, it doesn't make any difference. Jan is in prison, and if you want him, you must answer three riddles."

"Do you mean that if we answer the three riddles, you will let Jan go with us?" Raggedy Andy asked the Loonie King.

"Yes," the King replied. Then he told one of the Guards to bring Jan into the room. When the Guard returned with Jan, the Loonie King said, "Now I shall ask the three riddles."

"Let's see," he mused, "Why does a boliver bite biscuits? There's a hard one."

"I don't believe it is a riddle at all!" Jenny whispered to Raggedy Ann. "He's just making it up."

"I think so too," Raggedy Ann replied.

"What are you talking about?" the Loonie King asked.

"The boliver bites biscuits because he wishes to eat them," Raggedy Ann told the Loonie King.

"Good!" the King cried, "I mean, bad, for I do not wish you to guess them. Now! Why does a snickersnapper snap snickers from snuckers?"

"Isn't that silly?" the Camel with the wrinkled knees laughed.

"Don't you think that is a good one?" the King asked the Camel.

"Indeed, I do!" the Camel replied, "That is the Looniest one you have asked so far.

"I think so, too," the King replied proudly. "Now just you answer that one if you can. Just you answer that one!" he said to Raggedy Ann.

"The snickersnapper snaps snickers from snuckers because the snappersnicker snucks snickersnuckers from snuckersnappers snicker-snappers," Raggedy Ann replied, and it was all she could do to keep from laughing out loud. Raggedy Andy could not help it, he laughed so hard he fell upon the floor and rolled about.

"I don't see how you guess them so easily!" the Loonie King cried, "I never would be able to guess them myself!"

Of course, Raggedy Ann did not tell the Loonie King that she did not know the answers herself, for she knew that the Loonie King did not know the answers either, for he just made up the riddles as he went along.

"Now I have thought of a real, real hard one," the Loonie King said. "How can a hobgoblin hobble a gobble? Guess that riddle and I'll give you a fiddle."

"Anything you answer will be right," Jenny whispered. "The Loonie King does not know the answers himself."

"I know it," Raggedy Ann replied out loud.

"Then if you know it, why don't you answer?" the Loonie King cried.

"The hobgoblin can hobble a gobble by gobbling the hobble with a goghobblin," Raggedy Ann answered.

"Good!" the Loonie King cried, then remembering that he had not wanted Raggedy Ann to answer correctly, he shrieked, "No, I mean BAD! I did not wish you to guess my riddles so easily! Now I will have to ask you some more!"

"Oh, that isn't fair," Raggedy Ann said. "You promised if I answered three riddles, you would let Jan go away with us, so it wouldn't be fair if you did not keep your promise!"

"I've changed my mind now," the Loonie King

replied. "I shall ask you three more riddles; then if you answer them correctly, I will let you take Jan."

"No, sir!" Raggedy Ann replied. "You said three in the beginning. And I answered the three riddles. How do I know but what you might change your mind after I answered the next three?"

"Of course, you wouldn't know," the Loonie King said, "But that is just what I would do! I have a right to change my mind every time I feel like it, I guess!"

"Well, anyway," Raggedy Andy walked up to the King. "Raggedy Ann answered the riddles, so now we shall take Jan and leave you," he said.

"Ha! Ha! Is that so?" the King howled. "I shall see that you do not escape! Bring out the Looniest Knight I have. I shall have him cut off your nose!"

"Boo! Boo!" Raggedy Andy howled back at the King as loud as the King had howled at Raggedy Andy. Then the Loonie King stuck out his tongue at Raggedy Andy and before he thought what he was doing Raggedy Andy tweeked the King's nose so hard it made two large tears run out of the King's eyes.

Just then the Looniest Knight came galloping in, sitting astride a stick with a horse's head on the end. The Looniest Knight pranced up before the King and waved his sword, "Whose nose is

75

it, the Looniest King wishes cut off?" the Knight asked.

"There he is!" shouted the Loonie King, pointing to Raggedy Andy. The Looniest Knight rushed at Raggedy Andy and would have tried to cut off Raggedy Andy's nose if Raggedy Andy had not hurriedly crossed his fingers. The Looniest Knight did not know what to do when Raggedy Andy crossed his fingers, for you know, and of course everyone else knows, that means "King's Ex."

"What shall I do?" the Looniest Knight asked the King.

"You must fight!" the King cried. "Didn't you see him tweek my nose?"

"No, I didn't!" the Looniest Knight replied. "How did he do it?"

"Like this," Raggedy Andy laughed, as he tweeked the Looniest Knight's nose. Then while the Looniest Knight was wiping the tears from his eyes, Raggedy Andy awakened the tired old Horse and got upon his back. Then taking a long stick away from a Loonie man standing near, Raggedy Andy uncrossed his fingers. This was a sign that he was ready to fight.

Then the Looniest Knight jumped around with his hobby horse just as if he was on a real horse which was prancing about as if he could not guide it the way he wanted it to go.

"I believe he is afraid," Raggedy Andy laughed.

"He isn't afraid," the Loonie King said, "he just doesn't want to fight until he gets ready."

But although Raggedy Andy waited patiently, the Looniest Knight kept on prancing about just as if he could not make his hobby horse behave. Then finally, the Looniest Knight dropped his sword upon the floor and kicked up his heel and pretended that his hobby horse threw him.

"That wasn't any fight at all!" the Camel with the wrinkled knees cried. "The Looniest Knight was afraid of Raggedy Andy! That's what!"

"Sometimes he fights better than that," the Loonie King said. "Maybe he was afraid that Raggedy Andy would crack him with the long stick."

"Of course, I meant to crack him," Raggedy Andy laughed. "And I'll crack anyone who tries to keep Jan from going with us."

At this all the Loonies cheered loudly and the Loonie King came down from his throne and shook Raggedy Andy's hand. Then he shook hands with the tired old Horse who had gone to sleep standing up. Then he shook hands with Jenny and Jan and Raggedy Ann and the Camel with the wrinkled knees.

"You are so brave, I wouldn't think of keeping Jan any longer," the Loonie King told them. "So

you can all leave." And as our friends marched
out of the Loonie King's house with Jan, all the
Loonies ran after them shouting, "Long live the
brave Raggedy Andy! He vanquished the
Looniest Knight!" And even the Looniest Knight
and the Loonie King ran with them to the end
of the village, shouting with the rest of the
Loonies.

"Well," Raggedy Andy sighed when they had
left the Loonies behind at the edge of Loonie
Town. "I am mighty glad that is over! I never
was so frightened in my whole life!"

"Were you really?" Jenny asked. "Why, you didn't let on that you were."

"Of course not!" Raggedy Andy laughed. "If I had let them know that I was more frightened than the Looniest Knight, don't you see he wouldn't have been as frightened as I and would have cut off my nose," laughed Raggedy Andy. "And I didn't care to have my nose cut off, because then all my cotton stuffing would have leaked out and my head would have been as flat as a pancake."

"Well, here we are back at the tree," the tired old Horse said.

"Yes," Raggedy Andy added. "And I have been riding you all this time when you are so tired!" And Raggedy Andy jumped from the Horse's back.

"Really, I had not noticed it at all," the Horse laughed.

CHAPTER SIX

"Oh, wait a minute!" Raggedy Ann said, as they were about to enter the tree. "We do not want to go back up through the tree until we find Babette, the French doll! We must blindfold the Camel with the wrinkled knees and let him run backwards."

"Let's see," the tired old Horse thought out loud, "I will carry Jan and Jenny, while the Camel carries Raggedy Ann and Raggedy Andy. In that way we can get there quicker."

So Raggedy Ann again tied her hanky around the Camel's shoe-button eyes and after she and Raggedy Andy had climbed upon his back and Jan and Jenny upon the tired old Horse's back, the Camel started running backward lickety-split.

The tired old Horse ran just behind the

Camel's head and as Raggedy Ann and Raggedy Andy sat facing Jan and Jenny upon the Horse's back, they could talk comfortably as they rode along.

After they had galloped along for ten minutes, the Camel suddenly stopped and as the tired old Horse had been running with his nose very close to the Camel's nose, he bumped into the Camel so hard, the Camel's soft head was pushed way

back in wrinkles against his body, and Jan and Jenny went over the Horse's head and landed upon Raggedy Andy and Raggedy Ann.

"It is lucky you fell on us!" Raggedy Ann laughed, as Jan and Jenny got to their feet. "For Raggedy Andy and I are soft and it did not bump you much."

"It did not hurt us a bit!" Jan laughed as he brushed off Raggedy Ann's dress. "But how about the Camel?"

Indeed the Camel with the wrinkled knees did look very sad. His poor nose was flat and his neck was nothing but wrinkles. Jan and Raggedy Andy pulled and patted the Camel's head into shape again and it was not long until he looked as good as before.

"Why did we stop?" the tired old Horse asked.

"We ran into something," Raggedy Ann said, "but I can't see a thing." None of the others could see anything either, but when they felt in back of the Camel, they could feel an invisible stone wall. And although Raggedy Ann and Raggedy Andy ran along the wall for a long way, feeling it, they could discover no gate.

"There must be some way of getting in right here!" the Camel said, "for I am certain this is the exact spot I came out of."

"Maybe if you came out here there is a door, or gate there," Jan said.

"And maybe it only opens one way, like the stone at the room in the tree," Raggedy Ann suggested.

"But if that was so, I would have fallen through, just as the tired old Horse did," the Camel said.

"Oh, no you wouldn't," Raggedy Ann laughed. "For don't you see, Mister Camel, if you came out a door there, it must have swung out this way, and if you bump it from this side, it only closes that much tighter."

"That's so," the Camel agreed. "But can you feel any door knob?" Raggedy Ann had to admit that she could not, so there they were and could not get in.

After thinking for a while the tired old Horse finally suggested, "Let the Camel back up tight against the gate; for there must be a gate right here; and Raggedy Ann and Raggedy Andy get upon the Camel's back. Then the Camel can pretend that he has just come bouncing through the invisible gate and start to run. This may fool the gate into thinking the same thing and it may swing open as it would do just as someone passed through it."

"But it will close again," the Camel said. "Then we are just where we started from."

"Yes, but if the invisible gate swings open, I shall hold it open," the tired old Horse said.

"Then you can come back and we will all go through."

"It sounds reasonable," Raggedy Andy said, "let's try it, for there is nothing else to do." And he and Raggedy Ann climbed upon the Camel's back and the Camel squeezed back tight against the invisible gate. Then with a sudden spring, the Camel jumped away from the wall and ran a few steps.

"I've got it!" the tired old Horse called as he held the invisible gate open.

"How did you ever think of it?" the Camel asked, as he and the others walked through the invisible gate.

"I don't know," the Horse laughed. "I guess it was just plain Horse sense."

'Well, here we are," Raggedy Ann said, when they had all passed through the invisible gate. "And there is a queer little house built of sticks and stones and mud over there."

"I'll go over and see who lives there," Raggedy Andy said.

"We'd better all go," Raggedy Ann suggested. And so they all walked over to the queer little house. As they stood looking at it, a little old woman peeped slyly out of a crack in the door, then the door was opened wide and the little old woman came out. "Good morning," she said, "Can I serve you with any Witch-craft today?"

"I've never tasted any," the tired old Horse

replied. "But if it is anything which will keep me from getting so tired, I'd like to eat some."

"She doesn't mean food, Mister Horse, when she says Witch-craft," Raggedy Ann explained. "She means Magic!"

"Yes, that is just what I mean," the little old woman said. "I'm Winnie the Witch, and I serve people with Witch-craft. It is very cheap."

"How much is a nickel's worth?" the tired old Horse asked.

"Just five cents," Winnie the Witch replied. "What kind would you like to have, kind sir?"

The tired old Horse fumbled in his pocket and finally found a nickel and handed it to the Witch. "I'll take any kind you have, just so it is good for being tired," he said.

"Something in the shape of a bicycle pump?" the Witch inquired.

"He isn't an automobile," Raggedy Ann laughed. "What he wants is some hay, or oats, or corn that has been Magically made Magic to cure him of being tired."

"Yes, that is what I want," the tired old Horse agreed. "I don't care what it is, just so it makes me want to move quickly."

The Witch bit the nickel, then tinkled it upon her door step. "I just want to make sure it isn't lead," she said. "Yesterday a man came here with the loveliest doll and gave me ten cents for a bottle of Magic Medicine to make the doll come to life."

"It must have been the French doll, Babette!" Raggedy Ann and Raggedy Andy cried together. "And did you give him the Magic Medicine?" Raggedy Ann asked.

"Oh, yes," the Witch said. "But after he left, I tinkled the ten cent piece on the table and it was lead."

"He cheated you!" cried Raggedy Ann.

"Indeed, he cheated himself," laughed the Witch. "For whenever anyone tries to cheat me, whatever I sell them never does what they wish it to do. And so, you see, the bottle of Magic Medicine which I gave him turned to plain, everyday water just as soon as he gave me the lead dime."

The Witch, when she had finished telling our friend this, said, "Now we must all remain very quiet, while I work the magic charm for the tired old Horse." Then from her pocket she took a piece of red chalk and made a ring upon the ground. In the ring she drew many strange figures, each with a number beside it. Then she asked the Horse to step into the circle and shut his eyes. When he had done this, the Witch took a stick and gave the tired old Horse a crack upon his back. "Giddap!" she cried. And the tired old Horse jumped out of the circle and went scampering about with his head high in the air.

"There," the Witch said, with a sly wink at Raggedy Ann. "That was all he needed! In fact, anyone who is always tired needs the same thing, for they just imagine they are tired." Then when the tired old Horse came prancing back to his friends, he was so pleased he wanted all the rest to have some Magic too.

"I'm not a bit tired now," the Horse said. "I could carry all of you upon my back a long way now and not be the least bit tired! I could feel the Magic strike me all of a sudden," he told the Witch. "It was wonderful!"

"I haven't any nickels, or dimes," Raggedy Ann told the Witch. "But I wish that you could tell us how to find the man who had the doll. For we are in search of her and would like very much to find her and take her back home with us."

"I'll tell you a secret," the Witch whispered, after first looking all about her to make sure there was no one listening. "I do not care whether anyone pays me for working magic, or not. So,"

she went on out loud, "I will see what I can do
for you. Please step into the Magic Circle, all of
you."

"Shall we receive the same sort of Magic that
the tired old Horse received?" Jan asked. "I
wouldn't care to have Jenny get it."

"Now please do not worry about that," the
Witch promised. "You will not feel anything at
all." Then when they had all stepped into the
Magic Circle the Witch said, "You must all close
your eyes and count ten slowly. Then you may
open your eyes."

Raggedy Ann, Raggedy Andy, Jan and Jenny,
the tired old Horse and the Camel with the
wrinkled knees all counted slowly to ten, then
opened their eyes. Instead of the little house be-
longing to the Witch, which had stood a few feet
from them before, our friends saw a large tent
and coming from the tent were voices. Very

90

quietly they walked up to the side of the tent and listened.

"Ha!" one voice said, "The old Witch cheated me! The bottle of Magic was nothing but a bottle of rain-water! I shall go back and tear down her house!"

Raggedy Ann found a small hole in the side of the tent and peeped through, then she motioned the others to take a peep. There, sitting inside were twelve large men with black whiskers and long red noses. And each one had a large sword and two pistols in his belt.

"They are Pirates or something, I'll bet," Raggedy Andy whispered. "And there is Babette pretending she was only a doll and not moving at all! What shall we do? We must rescue Babette some way, but the Pirates are too large to fight!"

"They look very fierce," Jenny said. "Perhaps

they will capture us all and keep us prisoners."

"Listen," Raggedy Ann whispered. "They are talking."

"Ha!" laughed one of the Pirates. "I am about the bravest Pirate around here!"

"We are all of us the bravest!" all the other Pirates cried, each trying to say it louder than the others.

"How can we all be the bravest, I'd like to know?" the first Pirate asked.

"Because," one replied. "We are really not Pirates at all! So we all can be as brave Pirates as another!"

"That is quite true!" all the Pirates agreed, except the first one, and he seemed to be the Chief. "How can you prove that you are as brave as I am?" he asked.

"I know how we can prove which is the bravest!" one thin Pirate cried. "We can take twelve pieces of paper and put a spot on one piece, then we can put all the pieces of paper in the hat and draw. The one who draws the black spot can be shot by the rest of us. Then we'll put eleven pieces of paper in with one having a black spot and keep on until there is only one left and that will be me!"

"How can it be you?" the others all asked.

"Because I will mark the paper and remember which one it is each time," the thin Pirate said. "I shall be the one to mark the black spot!"

the other eleven Pirates cried. "For I want to be the last one left alive!"

"They'll be fighting in a few minutes," Raggedy Andy whispered, although it was not necessary for him to be quiet, the Pirates were quarrelling so loud they would not have heard had Raggedy Andy shouted.

Jan took a tin tube from his pocket and picked up some small pebbles, then whispering for his friends to keep still, he went around the tent until he found a small hole near one of the Pirates. Then with his tin tube Jan blew a pebble against a Pirate's cheek.

"Wow!" the Pirate howled as he jumped up and danced about. "Who hit me?" Then Jan blew pebbles against the other Pirates' cheeks until they were all dancing about, howling. Jan could scarcely blow the pebbles at the Pirates, he was laughing so hard, but when he could manage to straighten his face, he stung them with the pebbles. Then, not knowing what was happening to them, the Pirates all decided that it was safer outside the tent. And, each trying to get there first caused a jam at the doorway, and in a tangle of arms, legs and heads the Pirates fell in a struggling mass, pulling the tent down with them.

Jan immediately reached under the fallen tent, picked up Babette and carried her to where Jenny, Raggedy Ann, the tired old Horse and the

Camel with the wrinkled knees stood with Raggedy Andy.

The Pirates were struggling to their feet and there was no time to be lost. "Quick!" the tired old Horse cried, "Jan and Jenny upon my back and Raggedy Ann, Babette and Raggedy Andy upon the Camel's back."

94

This was done, just as the first Pirate got to his feet. And, seeing our friends running away, he knew in a moment what had happened.

With a loud shout to his companions, the Pirate started running after our friends. And as

the other pirates got to their feet, they followed. Then, as the tired old Horse and the Camel with the wrinkled knees could run very fast, the Pirates began shooting. Luckily, none of the Pirates knew how to shoot straight, so in a short time the Camel and the tired old Horse had left the Pirates far behind.

CHAPTER SEVEN

After the tired old Horse and the Camel with the
wrinkled knees had run for a long, long time, they
sat down to rest, and as they did not tell their
riders what they intended doing, Raggedy Ann,
Raggedy Andy, Babette, Jenny and Jan slid right
off onto the ground.

"I forgot to mention that I intended sitting
down," the tired old Horse said.

"So did I," the Camel chimed in. "It's funny
how I just took a sudden notion to stop and rest
just as the tired old Horse did."

"Well, no one was hurt," Raggedy Ann
laughed, "So please do not apologize."

"Babette is a lovely doll, isn't she?" Jenny
said as she smoothed the French doll's hair.

"Indeed she is," Raggedy Ann and Raggedy

Andy both agreed. "She's the prettiest doll of all."

"It's nice to have you say that, Raggedy Ann and Raggedy Andy!" Babette smiled so that her dimples showed. "But really, I must tell you that Raggedy Ann is the most beloved doll of all, isn't she, Raggedy Andy?"

"Yes, indeed that is true," Raggedy Andy told Jenny. "You see, Raggedy Ann is so old and so loppy and so generous and so kindly, and she can think so much better than any of us other dolls. And then, too," Raggedy Andy said, "Maybe you don't know it, but Raggedy Ann has a candy heart! Haven't you, Raggedy Ann?"

"Honest?" asked the Camel with the wrinkled knees. "Let's see it."

"Oh, it is sewed up inside my cotton-stuffed body," Raggedy Ann laughed.

"I thought maybe you had it in your apron pocket," the Camel said.

"Here, look," Raggedy Andy told the Camel. "You can feel Raggedy Ann's candy heart." And Raggedy Andy showed the other just where to feel. Even the tired old Horse was greatly surprised when he felt such a lovely candy heart.

"Were you frightened when the Pirate took you out of the playroom, Babette?" Raggedy Andy asked.

"Not a bit," Babette replied. "Only of course I did not wish to be taken away and I was afraid the Pirate would drop me and break my china head when he jumped over the fence."

"I thought you were a French doll," the Camel cried.

"She is," Raggedy Andy told the Camel. "What makes you think she isn't, Mister?"

"Because," the Camel said, as he scratched his head as if trying to figure it all out. "If she has a China head, she must be Chinese, so she can't be French." Everyone laughed at this and the tired old Horse turned a summersault and kicked up his heels with glee.

The Camel sat with a puzzled expression on his canton flannel face. "Well," he cried, "Just you tell me then. How can she be French when she is Chinese? Just you tell me that."

"How can a brick walk?" the Horse laughed. "Or a housefly?"

"I shan't answer your riddles unless you answer mine," the Camel said.

"Then I'll explain," the Horse started to say, when he saw in the distance a strange object bobbing up and down the ground and coming towards them. "Look!" he cried.

"It's a housefly!" the Camel cried, "I mean it's a flying house!"

"Indeed it is," Babette jumped to her feet, "It is the jumping houseboat of the Pirates! Run as fast as you can!"

The Camel with the wrinkled knees immed-

iately started running and the tired old Horse had to run after him and drag him back to the others by the string the Camel had for a tail.

"Now just see the time you've made us waste!" the tired old Horse shouted. "You know perfectly well that you and I must carry the others! Quick!" he cried. "Climb upon our backs!"

The Camel with the wrinkled knees couldn't think of anything to reply until he and the tired old Horse had run almost a mile, then he cried

to the horse, "Wait a minute! I just thought of something I want to tell you!"

"Tell me as we run along," the tired old Horse shouted back at the Camel. "Can't you see the Pirates are gaining on us every minute?"

"I just wanted to tell you not to be so bossy, Mister Tired Old Horse!" the Camel puffed as his black shoe-button eyes sparkled.

"Please do not stop to quarrel," Raggedy Ann said. "There is the Witch's little house right ahead."

"Shall we dash right in without knocking?" the Camel asked as he ran faster.

"Of course not," the tired old Horse replied as he also ran faster. "If the door is closed and we dash in, we would only break the door down and then the Pirates could dash in after us."

"The Pirates are right behind us," Jan shouted. "Hurry!"

Indeed, the Pirates' jumping houseboat was jumping right behind them when the Witch opened her front door and cried, "Run right in!"

The tired old Horse was the first in the door and the Camel with the wrinkled knees was right behind him. And they both came into the Witch's house so fast and it was such a small place inside, neither could stop although they braced their feet in front of themselves. The tired old Horse, Jenny and Jan, the Camel with the wrinkled knees, Raggedy Ann, Raggedy Andy and Babette slid across the floor and upset a large bowl of goldfish.

The witch slammed the door, "BANG!" right in the Pirate Chief's face, and the Camel cried excitedly, "I'm shot!"

Jenny and Jan picked up the bowl and replaced the goldfish before they had flopped very much, and the Witch ran to the kitchen and brought a pail of water to refill the bowl. By this time everyone had got on his feet except the tired old Horse, who had fallen in such a comfortable position he had gone to sleep.

The Pirate Chief banged upon the Witch's door with his sword. "Open the door, or I'll huff and I'll puff and I'll blow the house in!"

"Ha! Ha!" Raggedy Ann and Raggedy Andy laughed. "He has read that in a book! He can't huff and puff enough to blow the house in!"

"I'll soon show you!" the Pirate Chief howled. "You do not know what a good blower I am!" And he puffed so hard his eyes stuck out and it made him dizzy, but still he huffed and puffed! Then after huffing and puffing for six minutes, the Pirate Chief started coughing so hard the other Pirates had to pound him on the back. All those inside the Witch's house had been peeping through the chinks in the window-blinds, and when the Pirate Chief had to give up his huffing

103

and puffing Raggedy Ann and her friends laughed real loud and long.

"I know what we will do," the Pirate Chief said, after he had quit coughing.

"What will we do?" the others asked, as they crowded about him.

"We will lay a siege and starve them out! I've read in a book about how Kings often lay siege to a castle until the inmates are starved out!"

"But where will we get the siege to lay?" one Pirate asked.

"And besides!" another cried. "This isn't a castle!"

"Sillies!" the Chief cried, as he stamped around. "That doesn't make a bit of difference! All we have to do is to stay here until they get so hungry they come out and beg for something to eat!"

"That sounds like a good scheme," the thinnest Pirate admitted. "But won't we be getting just as hungry as they?"

"Of course not," the Pirate Chief replied. "We have a lot of things to eat in the jumping houseboat. And if we bring the food out here and eat it, that will make them hungry and very soon they will come out."

Now as everyone knows, Pirates are always very, very hungry. In fact almost as hungry as little boys, so they all ran to the flying boat and came out carrying bread and butter and dill pickles.

"Look!" the Pirates yelled to those in the Witch's house. "We've got something to eat! Yaha! Yaha!"

"That reminds me," the tired old Horse said as he got up and yawned. "I haven't had a bite to eat since I ate the violets."

"Snap Dragons," the Camel corrected.

"Violets," the tired old Horse replied very firmly.

"Yaha! Yaha! We've got bread and butter and dill pickles!" the Pirates teased outside.

"We don't care! We don't care!" Jan and Jenny called back.

"And we've got some sugar to put on our bread and butter, too, if we want it!" the Pirates yelled. "Yaha! Yaha! And you haven't!"

"Here we are," the Witch said; for, while the

others had been watching out the crack with hungry eyes, she prepared a lovely lunch with her magic charms. There were ham sandwiches, bread and butter and jelly sandwiches, pickles, ice cream, ladyfingers, doughnuts and watermelon. Everything looked so good it made tears come in Raggedy Ann's, Raggedy Andy's and the Camel's shoe-button eyes, for they had no mouths to eat with. And when the Witch noticed this, she took a pair of little scissors and snipped a mouth for each. Jenny and Jan and the tired old Horse, of course, were already sitting at the table with napkins tucked under their chins. All the time our friends were eating the lovely magical lunch the Witch had prepared for them, the Pirates were sitting outside with only bread and butter and dill pickles.

When everyone had eaten all they could, the tired old Horse said, "While you rest, for I know you are all sleepy from eating so much, I will 'red up' the table and wash the dishes." So the Witch, who was as sleepy as the rest, placed pillows around upon the floor and everyone laid down and took a nap. The Horse took all the cream puffs and ladyfingers and ham sandwiches that had been left on the plates to a side window and threw them out.

"Kittie! Kittie! Kittie!" he called and laughed softly to himself. All the Pirates came running to see what the tired old Horse had thrown out

the window. "Are your names all Kittie?" the
tired old Horse asked.

The Pirates saw all the nice things the Horse
had thrown out the window and said to each
other. "Just look at the goodies they have thrown
away, cream puffs and ladyfingers and ham
sandwiches and *watermelon!* My goodness! They
must have a lot of good things to eat if they can
throw away these nice things!

"And all we had was bread and butter and dill
pickles!" And the Pirates all had tears in their
eyes and mouths, for as you must surely know,

the tired old Horse had made them very, very hungry.

"We had the nicest lunch you ever, ever saw," the tired old Horse told the Pirates. "And if you promise to behave yourselves, I'll give you each a lollypop for I did not throw them away!"

"I'll promise," all the Pirates shouted, as they crowded about the window with outstretched hands.

The tired old Horse held out twelve lollypops. "Now if I give you each a lollypop you must promise to reform and not be Pirates any more. Now what will you be if you quit being Pirates?"

The tired old Horse held the lollypops so high the Pirates could not reach them.

"I'll quit being a Pirate and be a plumber!" one Pirate cried.

"And I'll quit being a Pirate and go in the garage business!" another shouted.

"And I'll quit being a Pirate and sell oil stock!" another cried.

"And I'll quit being a Pirate and be a—"

"Wait a minute!" the tired old Horse laughed, as he scratched his head. "I believe you had all better remain Pirates! So promise me you will be Pirates instead of driving taxi cabs, or going into the plumbing business or anything like that!"

When the Pirates had all said, "Cross my heart!" and promised, the tired old Horse gave them each a lollypop. Then one of the pirates began crying and handed his lollypop back to the tired old Horse. "What's the matter?" the tired old Horse asked, "Isn't your lollypop as large as the others?"

"Yes! Snub! Snub!" the Pirate sobbed. "But it makes me feel sorry that I took the doll away from its home. And I am ashamed to have you be so kind to me after I was so naughty." And the Pirate cried and cried as if his heart would break. In fact, he cried so hard, he got all the other Pirates to crying and they cried so hard, they could not eat their lollypops.

If it had not been so sad, the tired old Horse would have laughed, for the Pirates were all squawling in different keys and it sounded very strange.

"What is all the racket about?" the Witch asked, as she and the others came to the windows. "Did you put red pepper on the lollypops?"

"No," the tired old Horse replied, as he brushed away a tear and told his friends why the Pirates wept so loudly.

"I'll bet a nickel they have reformed," the Witch said.

"It isn't that," one of the Pirates said. "Charlie here is crying because he took the French Doll, and he knows that he was very, very wrong. And the rest of us are crying to think that one of our band would be so dishonest."

"Gracious!" the Camel with the wrinkled knees said. "I thought all Pirates were dishonest."

"Maybe they are," the Pirate Chief replied. "But you see, we were really not real-for-sure Pirates. We were just pretending that we were Pirates and that is why we all feel so sad about Charlie."

"And I feel sadder and sadder and sadder and sadder every minute," the Pirate named Charlie howled.

Raggedy Ann felt so sorry for Charlie and the other Pirates, she went outside and wiped

Charlie's tears away with her apron. "Now please do not cry any more, Pirate Charlie," Raggedy Ann said as she gave him a large fluffy cream puff with lots of cream in it. "We will forgive you for taking Babette and we know you will never do anything like that again."

Pirate Charlie smiled through his tears as he ate the lovely cream puff. "I'll tell you, Raggedy Ann," Pirate Charlie said, after Raggedy Ann had wiped the cream from around his mouth with her pocket hanky. "We always read stories about Pirates when we were little, and all of us decided that when we grew up we would become Pirates and sail through the air in a big flying houseboat. So when we finally grew up, we bought this jumping boat and pretended that we were Pirates. But all the time we longed for the things we should have had when we were children. And I always wanted a lovely doll. That is why I took the French doll."

By this time Raggedy Andy, the tired old Horse, Jenny and Jan and the others had gathered around the Pirates as they sat on the grass by the side of the Witch's little house. The kindly Witch brought out large dishes of ice cream for everyone and stood looking at the Pirates intently for a few minutes.

When everyone had finished eating their ice cream, the Witch, with a tinkly little laugh, said, "I want all the Pirates to sit in this circle!"

112

And she drew a circle upon the ground. When the Pirates had all taken seats inside the circle, the Witch placed a small red thing in the center of the circle and leading from the small red thing to the outside of the circle was a small rubber tube.

After the Witch had said a magic charm like this—"Hi Diddle Diddle, the Cat and the Fiddle!" only she said it backwards, she placed the small rubber tube in her mouth and started blowing. And, as the Witch blew, everyone saw that the small red thing was a red balloon, and it grew larger and larger until it was almost touching the Pirates' knees. Then the red balloon burst with a loud "Bang!" and everyone except the Witch was so surprised they fell over backward.

"Why!" the Camel with the wrinkled knees cried, when he got to his feet and looked at the Pirates. "They have had a magic shave!" Indeed, all the Pirates had lost their black whiskers and long red noses.

"They are all GIRLS!" Jan and Jenny cried in astonishment. The magic red balloon had blown the Pirates' false whiskers and false noses right off their faces. "Now girls," the Witch laughed, "You had better all come in my house and wash the red paint from your faces."

CHAPTER EIGHT

It is remarkable how black whiskers and false
noses and red paint will change anyone's appear-
ance. For, after the Pirates had had their false
whiskers and false noses blown off and had
washed the red paint from their faces, they were
all pretty girls.

"We even changed our names," the Pirate who
had been called Charlie said. "My name is
Charlotte."

The Witch picked up all the false whiskers and
long red false noses and took them to the Pirate
jumping boat. "Everybody climb on board," she
said. "For we will ask the Girl Pirates to take
us in the jumping boat to find Jan and Jenny's
mother and father."

"Why, how do you know about their mother,

Mrs. Witch?" the tired old Horse asked in surprise.

The Witch just laughed a tinkly laugh and took off her large hat. And with the hat came all her white straggly hair. Then she took off her long black cloak and stood before them a lovely girl not any older-looking than Jenny.

"Land sakes alive!" the Camel with the wrinkled knees cried. "She isn't a Witch at all! She's a Fairy Queen!" Everyone else was as much astonished as the Camel with the wrinkled knees.

"No," the Fairy who had been a Witch a moment before said. "I am not a Fairy Queen. I am only a Fairy Princess." And as the Fairy Princess waved her magic wand again the Girl Pirates' jumping houseboat became covered with beautiful fairy lights and started jumping along over the ground. It was just like sailing along over the water when the sea causes the boat to rise and fall with a gentle motion, and everyone enjoyed riding upon the Pirates' jumping boat.

"I thought it was funny that a Witch could be as kindly as you were," the tired old Horse said to the Fairy Princess.

"But one really can never tell by appearances," Raggedy Andy said.

"That is indeed true," the Fairy Princess laughed. "But so many persons always judge

people by the way in which they are dressed. Why, the ugliest shell may be hiding the most beautiful pearl and the roughest cover may be on the loveliest, sweetest story book. It isn't what is on the outside that counts; it is what we may have within us. But," the Fairy Princess laughed, "We must not conceal our good qualities, but must let others share them with us, for, whenever we give, then we most surely receive in return. And indeed, a heart filled with love within us always shines through in the kindly acts we do and in the sunshine we give to others."

The jumping boat had now reached the Land of the Loonies and jumped around their queer village towards the beautiful castle which stood upon the purple mountain beyond.

"Are we going to the lovely castle?" Jenny asked the Princess.

"Yes, my dear," the Fairy Princess replied. "For there we shall find your mother and father. And while we are sailing there I shall tell you their story. When they left you and Jan," the Princess said as she put her arm around Jenny, "they went to see your grandmother, and they intended coming back to you in two hours. But when they reached your grandmother's house, they found a lot of knights and courtiers; and indeed, they were very much surprised to find so many fine people there. And when the knights and courtiers saw your mother and father, they all fell upon their knees and cried, 'Long live the King! Long live the Queen!' And your father and mother discovered for the first time that your grandmother had been a queen, but her place had been taken by another woman whose soldiers had driven your grandmother away from the country. Now the other woman who had taken your grandmother's crown had been driven away by the knights who loved your granny and they had come to make her queen again. But Granny had been taken to Fairyland as the knights found when they came to Granny's little house, and they were just about to leave when along came your father and mother. So there wasn't anything to do except go with the knights and courtiers and be crowned King and Queen of the Purple Mountain."

"But why didn't Mother and Daddy send for us?" Jenny asked.

"That is the sad part of the story," the Fairy Princess replied. "You see, everyone thinks it is just lovely to be a King, or a Queen, for then, they imagine they can do just as they please and have everything they wish. But this is not always true. When your father and mother wished to return to their own little home, they found that they were not permitted to do so. For they were never permitted to step outside of the castle unless knights and courtiers went with them. Nor could they send anyone to bring you two children to them! And that is why I am helping you reach your mamma and daddy, for I know how they have longed for you!"

The Fairy Princess directed the jumping boat so that it came to rest in a beautiful garden of the lovely castle. And there sat Jenny's and Jan's mamma and daddy, the Queen and King of the Purple Mountain. Jenny and Jan, with whoops of joy ran and threw their arms about their parents. All the Pirate Girls and even the tired old Horse cried with happiness at the meeting.

"We shall get right in the jumping boat and leave with you," the King and Queen told the Fairy Princess. "For we never, never, care to be a King or a Queen again! The people here, if they wish, can have a republic, like the United

States of America; but we would rather be just plain, everyday folks in a plain, everyday house with plain, everyday people for friends!"

And so, the King wrote a note and pinned it to the chair, telling all the people of the Purple Mountain that he did not wish to be King any longer and that they might crown another King and Queen, or elect a President. Then the jumping boat jumped over the garden wall and sped away until the Purple Mountain and the beauti-

ful castle looked like a little toy far behind. The Fairy Princess served ice cream and chocolate cake to everyone on board, for she knew just how hungry they would all be after so much joy and excitement. So, with laughing and singing a board, the jumping boat finally reached the poor little house of Jenny's father and mother.

"Won't you all come in?" Jenny's mother asked. "The first thing I shall do after I take off my Queen's dress and jewels and get into a plain, everyday dress will be to make a whole lot of pancakes!"

"Whoopee!" the former King cried as he threw his crown up against the woodshed. "And I'll run out and chop a lot of wood to build the fire! I haven't had a chance to chop wood since I was King!"

"I do believe the neighbors have taken care of the chickens all the time we were King and Queen!" the mother laughed. "Bring in a hand-full of eggs, Henry," she called to the former King as he stopped chopping wood to moisten the palms of his hands.

"Gee! It sounds good to hear you call me Henry!" the king shouted. "I wouldn't be a King again for all the golden nickels in the world, Harriet!"

After Jenny's mamma had fried pancakes until they were stacked upon the table three feet high, and all the pancakes had disappeared, the

Pirate Girls told Raggedy Ann and Raggedy Andy and Babette that they would be glad to take them home in the flying boat.

"I really believe we had better be getting back," Raggedy Ann said, as she wiped her shoe-button eyes with the corner of her apron.

"Please wipe mine too," Raggedy Andy said. "I am sorry to leave such good friends, but what will Marcella think when she discovers that Raggedy Ann, Babette and I are not at home? She will think that we have been stolen."

"I can fix that all right," the Fairy Princess laughed. "I will show you when you get home."

The Camel with the wrinkled knees scratched his head a while and then said, "I have just thought it all over and I believe that the little boy who used to play with me has by this time grown up into a man, and he wouldn't care to play with me again, so I shall adopt Jan for my new master."

When the Camel with the wrinkled knees said this, Jan's father rubbed his eyes and picked up the Camel. As he turned the Camel over and over in his hands and wiggled the Camel's wrinkled knees, he cried, "Why, I believe, Harriet, this is a toy I owned when I was a little boy!" And so it proved to be, when he and the Camel told of different things that had happened years before. "Indeed, you shall adopt Jan!" the former king cried as he gave the Camel a fond squeeze. "And

the tired old Horse can adopt us too, if he wishes!"

"Indeed he can!" the former Queen cried. "And we will be most happy to have such a good friend!"

The tired old Horse tried to thank them all, but his throat seemed to be filled with lumps and he could only swallow real hard and blow his nose loudly. But the others saw a sunny light of happiness shining through his eyes.

After all had kissed each other goodbye, the jumping boat jumped away and in a short time everything began getting darker and darker.

"We must be going to have a terrible rain storm," Raggedy Andy said.

"No, no," the Fair Princess laughed. "That is not the reason it is getting darker and darker. You see, I am just sending the jumping boat back from today to yesterday night; which, when we get there, will be the same time that it was when you left."

Raggedy Andy rubbed his head thoughtfully, but could not quite make it out, so he remained silent. So did Raggedy Ann. When the flying boat came to rest in the back yard, Raggedy Ann and Raggedy Andy and Babette kissed the Fairy Princess and the twelve Pirate Girls goodbye

and ran through the grass and climbed into the playroom window.

All the other dolls were sound asleep, so Raggedy Ann and Babette and Raggedy Andy were as still as mice as they climbed into their dollie beds. Then after they had been quiet for a long time Raggedy Ann sat up and ran her rag arm through her yarn hair, then whispering to Raggedy Andy to follow her, Raggedy Ann and Raggedy Andy carefully crawled out of bed, climbed upon the window-sill and jumped "BLUMP" to the ground. Raggedy Ann picked herself up, shook the wrinkles from her dress and ran to the play-house, followed by Raggedy Andy. They jumped upon the doll-beds and bounced up and down as they smiled up at the wooden ceiling.

From outside came the songs of the little creatures who live in the grasses and the flowers and above these sounds Raggedy Ann and Raggedy Andy heard the "Squeek! Squeek! Squeekity-squeek!" of Johnny Cricket's fiddle as Johnny bounced up and down upon his seat on a tall blade of grass. And Raggedy Ann and Raggedy Andy did not feel a bit lonesome out there all alone, for Raggedy Ann and Raggedy Andy were thinking lovely, kind, beautiful thoughts. And when one is thinking lovely, kind, beautiful thoughts of course one has no time to become lonesome.

THE END